**Jeremy Strong** once worked in a bakery, putting the jam into three thousand doughnuts every night. Now he puts the jam in stories instead, which he finds much more exciting. At the age of three, he fell out of a first-floor bedroom window and landed on his head. His mother says that this damaged him for the rest of his life and refuses to take any responsibility. He loves writing stories because he says it is 'the only time you alone have complete control and can make anything happen'. His ambition is to make you laugh (or at least snuffle). Jeremy Strong lives in Kent with his wife, Susan, a cat or two, and something in the attic that makes scratching noises at night, but he hasn't found out what it is yet.

Some other books by Jeremy Strong

Jeremy Strong

There's a VIKING in my Bed

Illustrated by John Levers

PUFFIN BOOKS

PUFFIN BOOKS

Published by the Penguin Group
Penguin Books Ltd, 80 Strand, London WC2R 0RL, England
Penguin Putnam Inc., 375 Hudson Street, New York, New York 10014, USA
Penguin Books Australia Ltd, 250 Camberwell Road, Camberwell, Victoria
3124, Australia
Penguin Books Canada Ltd, 10 Alcorn Avenue, Toronto, Ontario,
Canada M4V 3B2
Penguin Books India (P) Ltd, 11 Community Centre, Panchsheel Park,
New Delhi – 110 017, India
Penguin Books (NZ) Ltd, Cnr Rosedale and Airborne Roads, Albany,
Auckland, New Zealand
Penguin Books (South Africa) (Pty) Ltd, 24 Sturdee Avenue,
Rosebank 2196, South Africa

Penguin Books Ltd, Registered Offices: 80 Strand, London WC2R 0RL,
England

www.penguin.com

First published by A & C Black (Publishers) Ltd 1990
Published in Puffin Books 1992
1

Text copyright © Jeremy Strong, 1990
Illustrations copyright © John Levers, 1990
All rights reserved

Set in Baskerville MT

Made and printed in England by Clays Ltd, St Ives plc

British Library Cataloguing in Publication Data
A CIP catalogue record for this book is available from the British Library

This edition has been produced exclusively for Nestlé Cheerios and
Honey Nut Cheerios

ISBN 0–141–31570–9

For Zoe and Tim – who else!

Contents

1 Crash Landing

Through the mist came the creak of many oars. Now and then there was a splash. The grey mist swirled and slid over the flat, grey sea, but not a sign could be seen of the boats: only the steady slap of oars and a few low curses.

Then a dark shadow moved within the mist, growing blacker as it came nearer, until the great wooden hulk of a Viking war-boat emerged, trailing wisps of fog along its sides. Twenty oars bit into the water, and forty Viking warriors strained over the heavy poles.

'Never have I seen a fog like this,' hissed the leader. He was a tall Dane, with a huge moustache and beard, fiery red. 'There is something I do not like about it.' He cast a glance at the lookout, standing up by the great dragon-head prow. 'Is there no sign of the fleet? Where are the other boats?'

The lookout sucked one finger and held

it up, as if to judge the wind direction. He stared into the mist, took off his helmet and pulled out both ears like radar scanners. His ears were big and red. The Viking leader cursed.

'Sigurd is an idiot. Why do we use a fool for a lookout?' Beside him, Tostig laughed. 'It's quite simple, Ulric. Sigurd can't row or cook. What else is there for him to do? You know what happened the last time he was at the oars. We ended up going round in a circle for almost an hour. And when he was cook, he boiled up all our best meat in a pot of seawater – urgh! At least he's safe up there.'

Ulric Blacktooth spat. 'Look at him, holding out his ears. What a fool!' He shouted forward. 'What can you see, Sigurd?'

'There's a lot of mist about,' answered the lookout. 'No, no, wait, there's something else. I can see something else through the mist!'

Ulric Blacktooth gripped the mast. Had they found the rest of the war-party at last?

'What is it? What can you see?'

'Wait a minute, the mist is clearing. Yes! I can see it quite clearly now.'

'What is it, what is it?' bellowed Ulric impatiently.

'There's water below, Ulric. I can see water. It's – the sea!'

Ulric Blacktooth shut his eyes and banged his head several times against the ship's mast. 'Tostig,' he hissed, 'that man will be the death of us all. Why are we cursed with such a fool?'

Tostig was snorting through his nose, a sure sign that he was losing his temper. Temper-losing was something that Tostig was very good at. He did it quite often – and practice makes perfect.

Now he drew his sword, which he had named Heartsplitter, and strode forward. In a moment he was beside the lookout.

'Sigurd, of course you can see the sea. We are on a boat. We are at sea.' Tostig spoke as if he wanted each word to hit Sigurd like a hammer. 'Now, Sigurd, if you wish to stay alive, do something useful! *Get yourself up that dragon's head, sit on top and don't say a word until you see the English coast. Do you hear?'*

So saying, Tostig thrust his sword (the pointed end) very close to Sigurd's backside. Sigurd gave a jump and scuttled up the prow, until he was right on the dragon's head. From there he turned and looked back at Tostig. 'I was only trying to help,' he complained.

Tostig grunted and returned to Ulric, while Sigurd sighed and tried very hard to see through all the mist that surrounded them. He was bored and tired. He had been on lookout duty for days. For some strange reason, nobody would let him row. Sigurd had always thought rowing was his best subject.

The boat was part of a large Viking raiding fleet, headed for England. They had been at sea for seven days, and the mist had been with them for the last twenty-four hours. It was a creepy, evil mist, making everyone nervous and jumpy. Somehow they had become separated from the rest of the fleet. Now they were drifting, they knew not where.

Sigurd strained his eyes to see through the swirling greyness. He pricked up his ears. What was that? Could he hear something? There was the splashing of the oars, but was there something else, perhaps the sound of breakers? Sigurd perched as far forward as possible, lying across the dragon's nose. He thought of shouting to

Ulric and Tostig, but they'd only be cross.

Sigurd stared and stared. The mist seemed even thicker. But the noise was louder now. It was breakers, surely? That could only mean one thing. They were close to land – maybe too close. Breakers meant a coastline, and that could mean rocks. He must tell Ulric. They were close to land at last.

'Ulric! Tostig! There's . . .'

At that same moment there was a sickening crunch and the long ship ran headlong on to low rocks. Sigurd was catapulted into the clammy English sea. The boat shuddered and stopped. Ulric picked himself up from the deck and shouted to the men.

'Reverse, quick, hard astern, go back, turn about! Full speed backwards!'

Twenty oars plunged into the sea, and the Vikings strained every muscle to move their boat off the rocks. Slowly the great wooden keel slid back. Slowly the sea caught hold of the long ship and pulled her clear.

'Back, back!' Ulric bellowed, as the warboat gained speed. 'Where's that idiot of a lookout?'

Tostig glanced at the dragon's head. 'Sorry to report, Ulric, I think he went overboard when we hit the rocks.'

Ulric was about to shout, 'Man overboard!', but stopped himself just in time. Sigurd overboard? What a relief! Ulric smiled. 'Full speed ahead, muffled oars,' he commanded, and the long ship slid silently away into the misty North Sea.

Sigurd was not happy. The English sea was wet and cold. This was something he had always suspected, and he was disappointed to find it true. Why hadn't they gone to the South of France for a raid? The sea was warm and blue there. Why did they have to come to grotty old Britain? He pulled a large piece of seaweed from beneath his helmet and waded ashore.

Sigurd stood on the beach. Cold salt water ran out of his helmet and down his spine. It trickled down his legs and filled

his boots. It was not a nice feeling. He
walked forward a few steps, slipped on a
dead jellyfish and fell flat on his back in a
rock pool. A large crab took an angry
swipe at one of his big red ears, then
marched away.

'Ow!' Sigurd scrambled to his feet. 'This
isn't my lucky day,' he muttered. 'Well,
there is only one thing to do. If the others
are not here to raid a village, I shall just

have to raid one by myself.' He drew his trusty (and rusty) sword, which he had named Nosepicker, and set off across the beach.

It did not take long to find the path up the cliffs. Indeed, Sigurd was surprised to find good steps cut into the rock face. He moved with all the stealth of a Viking raider, or so he thought. Here came the great warrior, eyes ablaze, sword drawn, soggy feet squelching in sodden boots!

The mist did not make things easier. It still clung to almost everything, and there was little that Sigurd could see. At last he reached the top of the cliffs and he followed the well-worn path ahead. He felt there were buildings near-by before he actually saw them. The path became hard beneath his feet. It was made of something he had never seen before. Sigurd's heart beat faster.

A cat ran yowling across his feet. Sigurd took a swipe with Nosepicker and almost chopped off his toes. Now he really could see houses. They were huge – much larger than he had expected. They had hard walls, and in the window spaces there was something he had never seen before. It was dark and shiny.

Sigurd peered more closely and suddenly saw a fierce warrior glaring back at him. 'Yargh!' yelled Sigurd and thrust forward with Nosepicker. There was a shattering sound and the enemy had gone. Sigurd leaped backwards. What kind of magic was this?

The mist was clearing all the time and Sigurd began to see such strange things. He could not even begin to describe them: there were no words in his language to do so. Things with wheels – yes, round wheels, but such small wheels, and certainly not made of wood. They were thick and black and had peculiar-shaped things on top.

Suddenly, two bright eyes appeared. Huge white eyes, glaring at him from the mist. There was a strange clinking sound. The eyes started forward. They stopped. They started again, and were getting closer and closer. Sigurd drew back into the darkness of a doorway. His shoulder pressed against something small and round.

'Bing-bong, bing-bong, bing-bong.' Every time he moved, the same weird sound went off in his left ear.

The bright eyes came closer still. A misty shape moved behind them, carrying something that clinked. The eyes whirred and moved away. Sigurd began to breathe more easily.

'Bing -bong, bing -bong.'

The door behind him began to open. Sigurd sprang to life and was off like a hare. He ran and ran, wherever the hard concrete paths took him. At one moment he saw those bright eyes again. They were moving much faster, coming straight at him and roaring angrily. Sigurd threw himself down a side path and one of those odd shapes on wheels rushed by. Sigurd stood there panting. He must find somewhere safe to hide.

He staggered up the path, his heart

pounding. Then all at once he stopped.
Right in front of him was a big picture: a
portrait of himself! There were the
moustache and beard. There were the
horned helmet and handsome nose. There
was Nosepicker, held aloft. It was himself,
no question.

Sigurd the Viking smiled and nodded.
There was some strange lettering
underneath which did not make sense, but
Sigurd didn't care. Surely this was his
home? He would be safe here at the sign
of The Viking. He grinned up at the

picture, mounted the steps, opened the
door and went inside.

Outside, the Viking on the sign almost
appeared to wink. The writing underneath
said:

THE VIKING HOTEL
Every modern comfort
MANAGERS: MR AND MRS ELLIS
Rooms available now

2 Double Booking

By eight o'clock in the morning, the mist had quite cleared and few people even realised it had been there earlier. The summer sun was now warming the pavements, and the sign outside The Viking Hotel swung a little on squeaky hinges. The Viking warrior did not seem quite so splendid in full sunlight. It was easy to see that the paint was peeling in many places. In fact, the warrior looked rather the worse for wear, as did the rest of The Viking Hotel.

Paint was flaking from the window frames. Plants were wilting in the flower troughs. Dust and litter had blown up against the corners of the walls and stayed there.

Mr Ellis fetched a broom and sighed. It was the same every day. He didn't know where the dirt came from, but it kept coming. He had washed the front windows only two days ago, and already they were smeary. It was no wonder there were hardly any guests at the hotel. It was the height of the summer season: the place should be full to bursting, but out of twelve guest rooms, only three were booked.

Mr Ellis swept the front steps clean and went back inside.

'Are you children up yet?' he called up the stairs. There was a distant reply of thumping feet. He went to help his wife get breakfast ready and lay the tables in the dining room.

Suddenly the staircase was filled with thunder. It shook and rattled as if an entire North American buffalo herd had decided to migrate down it. Zoe and Tim appeared breathless at the kitchen door.

'What's the matter, Mum?' Zoe asked, wondering why her mother was standing so still and pale. Mrs Ellis blinked.

'Oh, nothing. I just thought someone had fallen down the stairs. For a moment, just for a moment, I was seriously worried. I might have known it was you two getting up.'

'What's for brekkers?' asked Tim, grabbing a banana from one of the plates.

'Put it back. That's for the Ambrose boy, and you know how fussy he is. I don't know why his parents let him get away with it. You can have breakfast when you've laid the tables.'

Their father pointed to the dining room. 'Don't forget the small glasses for fruit juice.'

It did not take long to set the tables, with so few guests. As soon as they were finished, Zoe and Tim went back to the kitchen, where Mr Ellis was frying some eggs for them. He asked them what they were planning to do all day. Zoe looked across at Tim and shrugged.

'There is some shopping that needs doing,' suggested Mrs Ellis. 'Don't forget we have a new guest arriving this morning – Mrs Tibblethwaite.'

'Mrs what?' squeaked Tim.

'Tibblethwaite.'

'Fiddleplate?' Tim repeated, his small tongue struggling to go in three different directions at once.

'Oh, dear,' smiled Mrs Ellis, 'you'd better get it right before she arrives. Try again – Tibblethwaite.'

'Mrs Tiddlefate!' Tim jumped up with delight. 'There! I've got it, I've got it – Mrs Piddlegate!'

'Oh, Tim,' sighed Zoe. 'Come on, let's go and get the shopping.'

Mrs Ellis gave her daughter a list and asked her to see if she could get some sense into Tim before the new guest arrived. Mr Ellis watched them set off and then turned to his wife.

'I don't suppose he'll get it right. He's only five and it is a difficult name. Perhaps Mrs Tibblethwaite won't mind. Just think, we'll have four rooms booked!'

'Is her room ready?' asked Mrs Ellis.

'I did it last night. Honestly Penny, I don't know what we're going to do. We'll be completely broke soon. Nobody comes because the place looks like a dump, so we never make enough money to do it up again. It's a trap.'

Penny Ellis slipped her arms round her husband's waist and hugged him. 'Don't worry. Something will turn up.'

'You're right. Something has turned up – Mrs Tibblethwaite. And she's early. You finish off the breakfasts. I'll see to her.'

The latest guest was standing on the front step, looking at the hotel sign with some suspicion. She was a short, rather heavily built lady, with a large hat and even larger suitcase.

'Good morning,' cried Mr Ellis, flashing his best smile. 'You must be Mrs Tibblethwaite. You've arrived early.'

'Good morning,' replied the lady stonily. 'I always arrive early. You must be The Viking Hotel.'

'I'm Mr Ellis. Did you have a good journey?'

'No. The train was late: somebody

smoked in a no-smoking compartment so I pulled the alarm cord. The train stopped and I was fined fifty pounds because they said it wasn't an emergency. I told them it most certainly *was* an emergency if I was going to be forced to die of lung cancer. And then the taxi couldn't find this place at all.'

'I expect the driver took you to the Viking Cafe,' said Mr Ellis. 'They often make that mistake.' But Mrs Tibblethwaite was hardly paying any attention to him.

'We went to The Viking Cafe, The Viking Restaurant, The Viking's Delight, The Viking Chinese Take-away and The Viking Burgerbar.'

'Well, you're here now,' smiled Mr Ellis, seizing the heavy suitcase. 'Follow me, and I'll show you to your room.

'Just why are there so many Viking places around here?' asked Mrs Tibblethwaite, stomping up the stairs behind Mr Ellis.

'Ah, well, over a thousand years ago, Flotby was a favourite target for the Viking raiders from Denmark. There are lots of Viking relics round here and we have a Viking Festival at the end of every summer. Now, the bathroom is at the end of the corridor. You've got a lovely view of the sea from Room Four. The other guests are at breakfast now. Would you like to join them?'

'No thank you, I ate on the train. I don't know what it was. It arrived on a plate all wrapped up: I suppose they were afraid it might spread germs if it wasn't kept wrapped. Anyhow, I'm not hungry. What time is lunch?'

'That's at one o'clock. You'll see all the hotel details on the notice in your room.' Mr Ellis opened the door to Room Four and pushed the suitcase in.

Then he hurried back downstairs to help with the breakfasts.

'What's she like?' asked Mrs Ellis under her breath, as they passed between the tables pouring coffee and serving extra toast.

'She'll eat you for dinner. One gulp and you'll be gone.'

'Oh dear, all I need now is a difficult guest – as if the Ambroses aren't bad enough.'

At that moment, there was a loud cry from the top of the stairs.

'Mr Ellis! Mr Ellis! I say, Mr Ellis!'

Penny grinned at her husband. 'Oh Mr Ellis, I think that's your favourite guest, Mr Ellis. Do go and see what the matter is!'

'I'll give you "Mr Ellis",' he growled. He put down the coffee pot and hurried to the staircase.

'Mr Ellis,' cried Mrs Tibblethwaite, clutching the stair rail with one hand. Her face was white and trembling.

Mr Ellis took the stairs two at a time. 'Whatever is the matter?'

'Mr Ellis, there's a Viking in my bed!'

'What on earth do you mean?'

Mrs Tibblethwaite suddenly stopped shaking, drew herself up to her full (small) height and fixed Mr Ellis with two extraordinarily dagger-like eyes. 'I mean, Mr Ellis, that there is a Viking in my bed. What do you think I mean? If I say there is a Viking in my bed, I *mean* there is a Viking in my bed. Why don't you come and look for yourself?'

She grabbed Mr Ellis by one arm and hauled him off down the corridor. She kicked open her bedroom door and pushed Mr Ellis in front of her. He entered the room carefully and went across to the bed. No. There was nothing. Certainly the covers were all mucked up as if someone had slept there, but there was no sign of a soul.

'I think you must have been dreaming, Mrs Tibblethwaite.'

'I was not dreaming, Mr Ellis. There was a Viking in my bed. Good heavens man, do you think I don't know a Viking when I see one? He still had his helmet on. And his boots! I insist that you search the room.

Mr Ellis groaned. He got down on his hands and knees and looked beneath the bed. He pulled back the curtains and shouted, 'Boo!'

'There's no need to act the fool,' said Mrs Tibblethwaite coldly.

'There's nobody here,' said Mr Ellis, crossing to the wardrobe and pulling open the double doors.

A million coathangers seemed to burst from the wardrobe and a monster sprang yelling into the room, all arms and legs and hair. His black tangled beard had bits of seaweed hanging from it. His eyes glittered from beneath huge, shaggy eyebrows and a dented, two-horned helmet.

Sigurd snatched Nosepicker from the scabbard, glaring at the two strange creatures in front of him.

'Raargh!' he snarled, swishing Nosepicker through the air and slicing off a bit of curtain. 'Rrraargh!'

Mr Ellis simply stared, quite stupified. His brain had gone into shock. He could not move his tongue or lips. No sound would come from his throat. His feet felt as if they had been nailed to the floor. His arms were like lead sausage rolls.

Mrs Tibblethwaite poked him. 'There, you see? I told you there was a Viking in

my bed. Now, if this is some kind of
welcome committee, I don't think very
much of it. And if it's some kind of joke, it
isn't very funny. Don't just stand there, Mr
Ellis, do something.'

Mr Ellis did do something. He fainted. Sigurd gave a loud laugh and stepped towards Mrs Tibblethwaite.

'Oh no, you don't, you overgrown hairpiece. Take that, and that!' She began to beat the Viking with her handbag, almost knocking his helmet off.

Sigurd yelped, decided he'd had enough and ran from the room. He plunged down the stairs and almost fell headlong into the dining room, stopping himself just in time. He stood on the bottom step, panting and brandishing Nosepicker, while seven very startled hotel guests put down their toast and coffee and stared back at him.

3 Discoveries

Tim and Zoe walked into the dining room to discover their mother and seven guests huddled together on one side, while a strange hairy man glared at them from the other.

'Hello,' shouted Tim. 'Who are you? I like your sword.'

Before Mrs Ellis could make a grab at him, Tim was walking across the room, a big smile on his face. 'Is it a real sword or just plastic? I bet it's plastic.'

Sigurd watched Tim warily, but the boy was only a small child. He couldn't do any harm to a fierce Viking warrior like himself. Sigurd grinned back: he was a nice-looking lad.

'It is plastic, isn't it?' laughed Tim. 'That's why you're smiling. Come on, show me.' With that, he calmly reached out and took the sword from Sigurd.

It was difficult to tell who was the most

surprised. Sigurd was left empty-handed and unarmed. A five-year-old child had just taken his sword from him. Was he dreaming? No, because Tim had collapsed to the floor beneath the weight of the weapon. His eyes were popping.

'Wow! It *is* a real sword. A real, real, really real sword! Hey Zoe, it's a real sword!'

At that moment, Mr Ellis appeared at the top of the stairs with Mrs Tibblethwaite. Poor Mr Ellis was still in a state of shock. This was not surprising, because Mrs Tibblethwaite had spent the last three minutes trying to bring him round from his faint. First of all she had sat him upright and slapped his face several times. His cheeks were still red and sore. That hadn't worked so she'd begun to give him the kiss of life. At this point, Mr Ellis had woken up, found himself being kissed to death by Mrs Tibblethwaite and promptly fainted again, so the stout lady had jabbed him with her hat pin. That soon had him on his feet.

Now the pair were coming slowly downstairs, while Sigurd looked about in desperation. He was surrounded. He could not imagine where he was. This was a nightmare. None of the great stories of raids he had heard in Denmark had prepared him for anything like this. He had never before seen a room or people like these. Truly, this was some horrible nightmare he was in.

Sweat broke out on his forehead. The voices around him seemed to swim through his brain, echoing and gurgling. The walls of the dining room grew taller and taller until they started to bend in towards him, falling on him, falling . . .

Sigurd tottered forward and crashed unconscious across a breakfast table.

A glass of orange juice flew through the air, nicely sprinkling the guests as it passed overhead. A plate of egg and bacon spun off the table like some weird flying saucer. It deposited its passengers in an eggy mess on the carpet, then flew on, hit a wall and shattered.

Sigurd lay across the table, quite still.
There was a short silence and then
everyone started shouting and screaming
at once. Mrs Ellis rushed across and
hugged Tim, although he hadn't got a clue
why. Mr Ellis ran down the stairs calling
for calm.

'It's quite all right, everyone. Sorry
about the unexpected guest. He's obviously
some party-goer who had too much to
drink last night. If you wouldn't mind
going to the lounge, we'll clear up and

serve breakfast again in ten minutes. I do apologise for this most unexpected event.'

Mrs Ellis helped some of the guests out of the room, while Mrs Tibblethwaite stood at the top of the stairs, watching with one raised eyebrow. 'Do I understand, Mr Ellis, that you don't know this creature?'

'Of course not, Mrs Tibblethwaite.' Mr Ellis groaned as he tried to move Sigurd's heavy body from the table. His foot caught on a chair leg and the two of them crashed to the floor.

'Oh, for goodness sake!' cried the stout lady, marching down the stairs. 'Let me give you a hand.'

'Are you all right, Dad?' asked Zoe. There was a muffled reply and Mr Ellis crawled out from beneath the Viking. Together they turned Sigurd over so that he was facing the ceiling.

'What a mess. Look at him, drunk as a pig,' snapped Mrs Tibblethwaite.

'It's a brill sword, Dad,' cried Tim. 'Look!'

'It's a pretty good costume too,' Zoe added. 'It's so real. Pongs a bit, though.'

Mrs Tibblethwaite sniffed loudly. 'That's the drink.'

'I don't think so,' murmured Mr Ellis. 'Smells more like sea-water to me – and old food and damp leather.'

'Disgusting. He should be put in a bath at once.'

Mr Ellis thought for a moment. Penny asked if she should call the police, but her husband shook his head. 'This man is only drunk. I bet he'll have a splitting headache

– and feel very embarrassed – when he wakes up. We'll put him in Room Twelve, where he can sleep it off. Mrs Tibblethwaite, would you mind helping us get this Viking up to Room Twelve? I'm so sorry you found him in your bedroom. I can't think how it happened.'

Surprisingly, Mrs Tibblethwaite was now quite calm about the whole business. 'It's all right, Mr Ellis. Hotel rooms are usually such dull places. I must admit it was a shock to find him asleep in my bed, but at least it's something I shall remember for a long time. I'll take his left leg.'

It took five of them to carry Sigurd up the stairs to Room Twelve, and there they laid him out on the bed.

'Well,' said Mrs Tibblethwaite, 'all that excitement has made me hungry. Perhaps I'll have breakfast after all.'

'Of course. The other guests will want some too.' Mrs Ellis hurried back downstairs.

'I'm just coming,' added her husband. 'Tim, Zoe, stay here and keep an eye on this chap, will you? Come and tell us the moment he wakes up.'

Downstairs, The Viking Hotel returned to normal. All was calm in the dining room as the guests finally finished their breakfast, and soon the unwelcome visitor was forgotten.

However, things in Room Twelve were not calm at all. Just as Tim and Zoe were beginning to get rather bored with watching a sleeping body, Sigurd began to stir. He opened his eyes and tried to sit up. Then he clutched his head and fell back.

'He's got a headache,' said Zoe. 'Dad said he'd have a headache. Give him some water, Timmy.'

Sigurd took the water gratefully, and managed to prop himself up on a few pillows while he drank. He glanced at the two children and round the room. He felt for his sword, but of course it was gone.

Sigurd sighed. It was quite plain to him that he had been captured. Now he would probably be killed. There was no mercy for Viking raiders.

'Hello,' smiled Zoe. 'I'm Zoe. This is my brother, Timmy.'

'Tim, not Timmy,' grunted her brother.

'How do you feel?' said Zoe.

Sigurd listened to the strange noises being made by the children. He could not understand a word. Zoe was watching his face carefully. 'I don't think he understands, Tim. I don't think he's English.'

'Of course he isn't. He's a Viking, a real Viking.'

'Don't be stupid.' Zoe pointed at herself and said her name several times. Sigurd nodded. He pointed at himself, too, and repeated, 'Zoe, Zoe.'

'No, not you, *me*!' She took the Viking's hand and used it to point at herself. 'Zoe,' she said once more. Then she made Sigurd point at Tim and she said his name, too.

Sigurd's face lit up with a grin. 'Ah, Zoe!' he cried. Then he pointed at her brother. 'Timmy!'

'Not Timmy! Tim!'

The Viking pointed at himself. 'Sigurd,' he announced proudly.

Tim glanced up at the big warrior. 'Well, I'm going to call him Siggy,' he said moodily. The Viking banged his chest and glared back at Tim.

'Sigurd,' he repeated. 'Hedeby. Sigurd, Hedeby.'

'All right,' muttered Tim. 'Keep your hair on. If you want to be called Sigurd Hedeby, you can call me Tim Ellis. In fact, you can call me Master Tim Ellis.'

'Oh do shut up, Tim,' Zoe butted in, giving her brother a push. 'You do go on sometimes. Didn't he say Hedeby?'

'Sigurd, Hedeby,' nodded the Viking, and he started pointing all over again. 'Zoe, Tim, Sigurd, Hedeby.'

'*Master* Tim Ellis!' insisted Tim. 'Will you stop pushing me, Zoe!'

'You don't understand, do you, Tim? Sigurd keeps saying Hedeby, but it's not part of his name. I think it's where he comes from.'

'What do you mean?'

Zoe shook her head. Her face was pale and excited. 'We learned about Hedeby at school. It was a famous Viking settlement in Denmark.'

'But he is a Viking,' said Tim. 'So what's so special about that?'

'Hedeby doesn't exist any more. It was a Viking town, hundreds of years ago. It's not there any more, but here's Sigurd, and he says he comes from Hedeby!'

Tim groaned. 'Well of course he does. A real Viking wouldn't come from anywhere else, would he? I told you he was a real Viking!'

4 Lunch – Viking Style

Tim and Zoe's parents were reluctant to listen to their story of the real Viking in Room Twelve, let alone believe it. The children had to wait until all the breakfast things had been cleared away, and the washing-up done. Then Zoe dragged her parents up the two flights of stairs to Room Twelve, where Tim was busily trying on Sigurd's helmet.

The Viking was very worried when Mr and Mrs Ellis appeared. He still thought he was due for execution. But Zoe reassured him by introducing everyone. Her father felt rather foolish saying, 'Good morning, Sigurd,' and shaking hands with a Viking. But Sigurd was proud of his own party piece: 'Sigurd, Hedeby, Denmark.'

Mrs Ellis shook her head. 'He's just pretending. He must be English. He doesn't want us to know who he is so he can't be charged for all the damage he's caused.'

Zoe had fetched some drawing paper and pencils. She sat down on the edge of the bed and sketched the whole Ellis family, writing their names underneath.

'Hey, that's not me,' Tim complained. 'I'm not fat.' Zoe ignored him, and all the time she drew, she told Sigurd what she was doing. 'This is me, this is my dad, Mr Ellis . . .' And so she went on. She drew the hotel and the sign. Sigurd pointed to it excitedly. Finally Zoe stopped and gave him the pencil.

He stared at the thin piece of wood as if it was something magical. It was quite plain that he had never seen a pencil in his whole life. Zoe looked up at her parents. 'See?' she said.

'He's kidding us,' muttered her father.

Siggy now began to make a few practice strokes with the pencil, then slowly and carefully he started to draw. The others crowded round the bed. A tense, fascinated silence descended on them. Siggy's story slowly took shape on the paper. He drew his house and the longships, including an ugly and fierce-looking warrior with a vast beard. (This was Ulric Blacktooth and it was a good thing that Ulric wasn't around to see it.) He drew the ships setting sail, the mist and how he'd fallen into the sea.

'Now do you believe us?' Zoe asked in a whisper, as Sigurd put down the pencil and looked at them all in turn.

Mrs Ellis hesitated. 'I really don't know, dear. I mean, you must admit, it doesn't seem all that possible.'

Her husband grunted. 'I'm fed up with this play-acting. This man is no more a Viking than I am. He's just some left-over drunk from a fancy dress party.' He turned to Sigurd and felt his rough leather jacket. 'I bet you he's got his driving licence on him somewhere – and all his credit cards. That will prove who he is.'

Tim giggled. 'Vikings don't have driving licences!'

'He's not a Viking!' shouted Mr Ellis, standing up. 'I'm going to ring the police. He's bound to have been reported missing.'

But nothing of the kind had happened. Two very polite policemen came to the hotel. They asked Sigurd several questions, which of course he didn't understand. They searched his clothes and found nothing but a few seashells and a small dead crab. They told Mr Ellis that, as far as the police were concerned, there was little they could do. Then they left.

'Does this mean we can keep him, Daddy?' asked Zoe.

'Zoe! We're not talking about some pet animal. Sigurd is a human being – I think. I suppose he'll have to stay here until we find out more about him.'

'Another mouth to feed,' Mrs Ellis complained.

'Yes. Well, he'll just have to work for his living. He can help in the kitchen with the washing-up.'

'I suppose he's probably hungry now,' said Mrs Ellis. 'We'd better take him down for lunch. He can sit in the corner of the dining room.'

'Are you hungry?' Tim asked brightly.

Sigurd frowned. 'Oh, you know, Siggy. Food, nosh, lovely grub – din-dins.' Tim's father rolled his eyes at the level of this intelligent conversation. Siggy still didn't understand, not until Zoe pretended she was eating. Then his eyes lit up and he banged his stomach with both fists. He made a sweeping circle with his hands, as if to show that he had an enormous appetite.

'That's what I was afraid of,' said Mrs Ellis, as they went downstairs.

The Viking had not eaten for more than twenty-four hours, and he glared at the other guests in the dining room as if he would have liked to swallow *them*. The Ambrose family were so put off that they hid behind their menu cards, whilst their charming son, Roger, did a few experiments to see how long it took to empty the salt cellar into the water jug.

Siggy stared at the clean white tablecloths and napkins, the placemats and cutlery. Most odd, he thought. He picked up a table knife, ran his thumb down the blade and threw it to the floor. What a useless knife! You couldn't kill a grasshopper with something as puny as that.

Zoe brought in some roast chicken and put it on the table. As she turned her back to fetch the vegetables and gravy, Sigurd seized a chicken leg and ate it in three seconds flat. He tore the meat off with his teeth and threw the bone over his shoulder. It disappeared half-way up the stairs, bounced off the banisters and hit Roger on the back of the head.

'Ow! I wasn't doing nothing!' muttered Roger, thinking his father had just clipped him round the ear.

When Zoe returned with the gravy, Siggy took the gravy boat and began to drink straight from it, mistaking it for beer. He took two huge swigs. His eyes almost exploded, his cheeks swelled up and he spat the whole lot out over the tablecloth.

'Siggy!' Zoe cried. 'What on earth did you do that for?'

'Urgh, urgh,' said Sigurd, drawing his sleeve across his mouth.

The other guests watched with horror.
Mrs Ambrose bent over her son and
whispered in his ear. 'Don't think you can
behave like that, Roger. The man's a
monster.'

Zoe tried to put some Brussels sprouts
and carrots on Sigurd's plate, but he swept
the whole lot to the floor. He wanted meat
– and lots of it. He pushed back his chair

and went to all the other tables, seizing
any chicken that was left and cramming it
into his mouth.

'Hey,' cried Mr Ambrose. 'That's my
chicken!' He tried to grab Sigurd's arm,
but the Viking growled and fixed him with
such a fierce stare that he meekly put his
hands in his lap.

'You're a coward, Herbert Ambrose,'
hissed his wife. 'You've got to stand up to
him. Ask him for your chicken back!'

'But he's eaten it!'

'Huh, any excuse! You're just a wimp. I
always knew you were a wimp. You were a
wimp when I married you and you're still
a wimp.'

Poor Mr Ambrose was bright red and
slowly turning purple. 'If I'm a wimp then
you're a . . . you're a squidface!' he blurted
out – and seeing the look of shocked
surprise on his wife's face, he went on.
'You were a squidface when I married you
and you're still a squidface.'

Now he was laughing hysterically. His
wife picked up her fork and jabbed at him.

Zoe had already rushed back to the
kitchen to fetch help, and her parents
came hurrying into the dining room to sort
things out. Siggy had just swiped the last
of the chicken from the guests. The floor
was littered with bones. Mr Ambrose was
standing on a chair, shouting 'Squidface!'
at the top of his voice; his wife was
bombarding him with sprouts and carrots;
Roger was hiding beneath the table,

drinking boatfuls of gravy and seeing how far he could spurt them out again.

Surprisingly, it was Mrs Tibblethwaite who came to the rescue. All this time she had been sitting in the far corner of the room, sternly watching everything. Now she rose to her feet and pushed back her chair.

'This has gone on quite long enough,' she announced. 'You ought to be ashamed of yourselves.' She marched across to Sigurd, grabbed him by the beard and led him back to his seat. Then she crossed to Mr Ambrose, yanked him from the chair and slapped his face, twice, pushing him into his place. She also slapped Mrs Ambrose across one cheek. Finally she reached under the table, hauled Roger out by the ear, gave it a good tweak and sat him down, too.

This was followed by a shocked silence, during which four people clutched their faces and watched Mrs Tibblethwaite warily. She glared back at them, breathing heavily, hands on her hips.

'I have never seen such behaviour at a dinner table in my life! Anyone would think this place was a zoo. Look at the state of this room. It must be cleared up at once, and you – all of you – are going to clean it!'

Mrs Ambrose choked. 'He started it,' she blurted out, pointing at Sigurd.

'That man is a Viking warrior,' said Mrs Tibblethwaite. 'How else do you expect him to behave? He doesn't know any better – but you do. Now start cleaning. Tim, fetch me Sigurd's sword!'

Tim ran from the room and quickly returned with the mighty weapon. Mrs Tibblethwaite took it and stood over the Ambroses as they got to work with mop and bucket.

'As soon as this is done, we're leaving!' hissed Mr Ambrose. 'This is the worst hotel we've ever stayed in. It's chaos and we're treated like slaves.'

'Just work and don't backchat,' warned Mrs Tibblethwaite, prodding him with Nosepicker.

Mr and Mrs Ellis had slumped into chairs in the kitchen.

'What are we going to do? That's three paying guests gone and one extra guest who squirts gravy everywhere. Oh Keith, we shall be ruined. We'll never have enough money to put things right!'

Her husband's face was stony. It was all too true. The kitchen door swung open and Mrs Tibblethwaite strode in.

'And what do you think you're doing, moping in here? Haven't you got a hotel to run? Come on, get on with it. People are still waiting for their lunch out there, and I don't suppose Sigurd has finished eating yet. You get some sausages cooking, while I sort out more vegetables. Come on, get cracking!'

5 Great Changes

The next few days seemed to pass in a haze. So many things happened that the Ellises could hardly keep pace. First of all they had to cope with Mrs Tibblethwaite and Sigurd. It was impossible to say which one was worse. Mrs Tibblethwaite seemed to have changed from being a guest to becoming one of the hotel managers. She was everywhere – ordering people about, cleaning, polishing and cooking. And although she got on everyone's nerves, it had to be admitted that she was a great help. Mr and Mrs Ellis would probably have given up if it hadn't been for her.

Siggy was like a giant, hairy child. His first ride in the car was remembered by most of Flotby. This was probably because he was so excited that he climbed out of the window and stood on the roof, waving Nosepicker and shouting to everyone, 'Good morning, how do you do?' (Zoe had taught him those words only the previous day, and he was still practising.)

Then there was the Viking's first bath. Zoe tried very hard to explain what he was meant to do. She ran a nice big hot bath. She showed him the soaps and shampoo. She acted out what bathing was all about. Then she pushed Siggy into the bathroom and shut the door. A few minutes later, she heard splashing and singing, and she happily went downstairs to report that all was well.

Five minutes passed, and Siggy appeared in the lounge. He was dripping wet, but still had all his clothes on: he'd smeared them with soap and shampoo. Shiny, multicoloured bubbles slowly slid down his chest and legs and popped from his armpits. For some strange reason he'd stuck a bar of soap on to each helmet horn.

'I don't think he understood me properly, Mum,' Zoe murmured.

Most spectacular of all was Sigurd's first attempt at helping out in the hotel. Mr

and Mrs Ellis made him follow them
round for a whole day, showing him what
they had to do. He watched them vacuum.
He picked up the pipe and put it to his
face, only to have his beard sucked down
it. Sigurd roared and ran off, dragging the
vacuum cleaner behind him, until the plug
was wrenched from the socket; the machine
then stopped and the pipe released his
beard.

Sigurd watched all the dirty sheets and towels go into the washing machine. He sat amazed while they spun round and round. He examined them carefully when they came out and flashed a broad smile at Zoe.

'Clean!' he said, and nodded with delight.

'He's learning ever so fast, Dad,' said Zoe.

'Good, he can do the washing up, then,' said Mr Ellis snappily – for this was the job he hated most of all. Besides, he was in a bad mood, still brooding on the problems of running a hotel with hardly any guests and a lot of bills to be paid.

The dirty dishes were piled up by the kitchen sink. Mr Ellis pointed at them. 'Sigurd, you clean? Understand?' Siggy came over to the sink. He picked up a dirty plate. Mr Ellis repeated his order. 'You clean. Understand?'

Sigurd gave a grin and nodded. 'I clean. I understand. I clean plips.'

'Not plips – plaps. No, I mean plates,'

said Mr Ellis wearily, and he went off to clear the tabletops.

'I clean plaps,' muttered Siggy to himself, looking round the kitchen. He gathered up an armful of dirty crockery, opened the washing machine and put it all inside.

'Clean plaps very quick, easy peasy,' said Sigurd as he switched the machine on. He pulled up a chair and sat down to watch.

The machine filled with water. It began to rotate. The plates started to clatter against one another. Something broke. Something else cracked. The machine stopped. Siggy stared at it. He was about to open the door, when the things inside rotated the opposite way. There was a dreadful clatter and scrunch. An awful grinding noise came from the machine, along with the merry sound of tinkling glass and dozens of plates breaking into tiny pieces.

Sigurd sprang to his feet. This was certainly not meant to happen. He shouted at the washing machine. 'No, no!

You clean, you clean plaps!' He punched the controls helplessly and started the spin programme. Faster and faster whirled the crockery, while Sigurd tugged at his beard in anguish.

Just as Mr Ellis came running to the kitchen to see what all the noise was, Siggy opened the machine door. Fragments of china came flying out at high speed, along with several gallons of soapy water. Mr Ellis screamed, raced to the power plug and switched off. The machine ground to a halt.

Siggy stood up in a deep puddle, from which poked a hundred bits of broken plate, sticking out like the hulls of sinking ships. He bent down and picked up a fragment. He looked at it dolefully and said with some sadness, 'Plaps gone small.'

'I'll give you plaps, you overgrown hairy meat ball!' shouted Mr Ellis. 'Look what you've done! Look!' He seized a carving knife and began to advance on the Viking, who backed towards the door. 'Get to your room at once and stay there! Don't you

dare come out until I say so. Do you hear?
Now MOVE!'

Whether Siggy understood the words, or
just reacted to the knife, it's hard to say,
but he ran up the stairs four at a time and
barricaded himself into Room Twelve.

The episode with the washing machine
was followed by a big conference within
the Ellis family. Mr Ellis kept saying that
Sigurd would have to go: they simply
couldn't afford to keep him in the hotel,
which was losing enough money already.

Zoe and Tim were almost in tears,

especially when their mother said she thought their father was right. 'Too many things go wrong when Sigurd's around,' she added.

'But where will he go, Mum?' Zoe sniffed. 'You can't put him out on the street.'

'No,' snapped Mr Ellis. 'But we can jolly well put him on a boat and send him back to Denmark.'

Everyone stopped and stared at Mr Ellis. 'Don't look at me like that,' he said. 'I'd like to know why not? That's where he came from. He rowed over here – he can bloomin' well row back. Come on!'

A strange procession made its way down to the beach. Tim and Zoe tugged at their father, trying to get him to change his mind. Mrs Ellis kept repeating that it had to be done. Besides, Siggy would be so much happier at home in his own country. As for Siggy himself, he didn't know what all the shouting was about, and was much more interested in all the boats in the harbour. He pointed at them and said a lot in his own language.

'See?' said Mr Ellis. 'He wants to go home.' He fished a handful of money from his pocket and paid for the hire of a large rowing boat.

'How long for, mate?' asked the owner.

'How long does it take to row to Denmark?' muttered Mr Ellis darkly.

'What's that?'

'Just keep the change,' snapped Mr Ellis. He pushed Sigurd into the boat and thrust the oars at him. 'There. Denmark is that way,' he said, pointing out across the open sea. 'Start rowing!'

Siggy nodded happily and grabbed the oars. This was wonderful. 'Siggy go home.

Hedeby! Goodbye, so long, how do you do!' The boat slowly moved out through the first few waves. 'I go. No more plaps. No more bathpoo.'

'Shampoo,' Zoe corrected tearfully. The rowing boat was now some distance away, and steadily getting smaller. Its path through the waves was a bit crazy, but it was moving out of sight.

'Bye, Siggy,' whispered Tim. Zoe reached down and held her brother's hand tightly.

Mr Ellis watched grimly until the rowing boat was out of sight. Penny Ellis slipped an arm round his waist. 'Do you think he'll be all right?'

'Of course. He's a Viking – born to the sea. Those Vikings sailed to North America, right across the Atlantic Ocean. This time tomorrow, he'll be safe at home.'

Mrs Ellis sighed. 'You know, in a strange way, I shall miss him.'

'I won't,' grunted her husband, and they made their way back to the hotel.

On their return, Mrs Tibblethwaite

came hurrying down the front steps to
meet them.

'There you are! I am so glad you're
back. Now, there's a family in the lounge.
They want to know if you have any rooms
vacant, as they wish to stay for two weeks.
I must say, they seem very nice. And there
are children, so Tim and Zoe will have
people to play with. They're very excited
and dying to meet Sigurd.'

'Sigurd?' repeated Mr Ellis. 'What do
you mean, dying to meet Sigurd?'

'They saw him in Flotby, standing on a
car roof and waving a sword. They seem
to think it was some kind of advertising
stunt. I told them he was a real Viking:
they don't believe me, of course, but they
will as soon as they meet him. Anyhow, the
children are pestering their parents to let
them stay at the hotel with the Viking, so
here they are. But where's Siggy? They
won't wait much longer, you know.'

Mr Ellis slumped into a chair and closed
his eyes. He couldn't believe his bad luck.
Surely this couldn't be happening to him?

When he opened his eyes, the first thing he saw was Tim and Zoe watching him, their faces full of accusation.

He leaped to his feet and raced down to the beach. 'Siggy!' he yelled. 'Come back! You can come back, Siggy – please!' Mr Ellis stared out across the grey water to the endless horizon. There was nothing to be seen but waves and a few gulls circling slowly in the empty sky.

6 A Present from Thor

How do you explain to four excited children and their parents that you have just got rid of a real Viking? Mr Ellis winced and began. 'You see, we did have a real Viking. His name was Sigurd and he arrived from nowhere. We don't know how or why. Mrs Tibblethwaite found him in her bed. Then he hid in the cupboard, you see . . .' his voice trailed away. The story sounded so unreal, he could hardly believe it himself. Mrs Ellis carried on.

'He put the cups and saucers in the washing machine, drank gravy by the boatful and stuck the soap on his helmet, so we put him in a rowing boat and now he's rowing back to Denmark.'

'By himself?' asked Mrs Tibblethwaite in surprise. 'Really, Mr Ellis, I'm rather shocked.'

'It wasn't an advertisement then?' interrupted Mr Johnson.

'No.'

'He was a real Viking but we can't see him because he's rowing to Denmark?'

'Yes.'

'And you expect us to believe all that?' Mr Johnson sat and grinned at them all. 'Come on, you're joking, and it's a pretty good joke too.'

Mrs Tibblethwaite grunted and drew herself upright. 'It is no joke, Mr Johnson. I believe it because I know it is true, and I expect you to believe it too. I have been staying at this hotel for a week, and so has Sigurd. I know him very well.'

Mrs Johnson stifled a giggle. 'Oh I see – Mr Sigurd is your husband?'

'Of course he isn't!'

'But he was in your bed?' Mr Johnson added.

'Yes, I mean no – yes! Look, are you calling me a liar?' demanded Mrs Tibblethwaite angrily.

'No,' replied Mr Johnson. 'But you might be a nutcase. Surely you don't really think this character was a real Viking?'

Mrs Tibblethwaite sat down in despair. Mr Ellis started to say that obviously nobody was likely to believe them. Perhaps it was best if the Johnsons left. After all, Sigurd had gone.

He was half-way through this speech, when there was a heavy thudding and a clatter from the hallway. It sounded as if half an army had just broken down the front door and ridden into the hall. Zoe was about to go and investigate when the door burst open and Siggy squelched in. He was soaking wet and clutching a long piece of rope that trailed out of the room. Several bits of seaweed flapped about the horns of his helmet.

'Siggy!' cried Zoe, hugging him, even though he was wet.

'Siggy, Siggy!' Tim yelled, climbing up his dripping leg. 'Yuk!' he added and quickly let go.

'It's the Viking!' screamed all the children.

'How do you do, good evening, it's a lovely yesterday,' said Sigurd, beaming from ear to ear beneath his beard. 'I go row Hedeby. I row and row, round and round. Boat go this way, boat go that way. Where am I? Only water, no land, can't see. I stand up to see better. One oar go away.'

'What does he mean, "One oar go away"?' asked Mrs Johnson.

'He lost an oar,' Zoe said quickly. 'Go on, Siggy. Then what happened?'

'I row and row, one oar, I go round in circle, only smaller. I stand up again . . .'

Mr Ellis groaned. 'Don't tell me, you lost the other oar.'

Sigurd shook his head and drops of sea-water sprinkled from his beard. 'No, I keep oar, but fall into sea, splishy-splashy. Climb into boat but boat fall over, slopsy-wopsy. Boat sink. I sink. Gurgle-gurgle.'

'Good grief, who taught this idiot to speak?' moaned Mr Ellis.

'I swim. I reach land. I come here.' Sigurd stopped and grinned madly at everyone. 'I bring present. Present for Mr Ellis and Mrs Ellis.'

'A present?' repeated Mrs Ellis weakly.

'To say thank you and how are you,' explained Siggy. He hauled on the rope in his hand. There was a strange clumping noise beyond the door. Sigurd pulled harder and at last brought into the room a large black and white cow. It stood there next to the settee like an alien from a distant planet, watching everyone with vast, moony eyes.

'This for you,' Sigurd said to Mr Ellis. 'Present from Thor, God of Thunder. We make offering.' Siggy pulled Nosepicker from his scabbard. 'Tonight we kill cow to say thank you for safe return and I not drown.'

One of the Johnson children was hiding behind her father. The youngest one was holding his nose and pulling at Mrs Johnson's sleeve.

'Mummy, mummy, I think that cow has just done a . . .'

'Yes dear,' interrupted Mrs Johnson quickly. 'I know.'

'Tonight we have feast,' Sigurd went on. 'Lots to eat. Yummy.'

Mr Ellis sighed heavily. A few minutes earlier, he had wished Sigurd was still with them. Now the Viking was back and already Mr Ellis was wishing he'd gone down with the boat, gurgle-gurgle.

'Zoe, please take Siggy and that cow outside,' he said. 'Explain why we can't sacrifice cows, and for goodness sake find out where this one came from. Take it back before some farmer slaps us all in jail. I shall try and sort out things here.'

Mr Johnson had started to laugh. He got up from his chair and seized Mr Ellis by the hand, pumping it warmly. 'I have an apology to make. I certainly do believe you. That Siggy must be a real Viking, couldn't be anything else. He's either a Viking or the biggest banana-brain I've ever met. Anyhow, I think it's fantastic. Question is, have you got a room for my family? We'd love to stay with a real Viking, wouldn't we?'

Mrs Johnson looked at the mess on the lounge floor. 'Only if the cow goes.'

Mr Ellis hastily began to push the bemused cow backwards out of the room. 'Of course, no problem. This cow hasn't paid its bill for weeks, anyway,' he joked.

Mrs Tibblethwaite let out a long sigh while Mr Ellis and Zoe rushed off to fetch keys and prepare beds. She could see how busy they were, so she quietly set about cooking supper for everyone.

By the time bedtime arrived, the Ellis

family were exhausted. Mr Ellis kissed his children good night. 'I have an apology to make, too. I'm sorry I put Sigurd on that boat.'

Zoe hugged her father tightly. 'That's all right, Dad. He's come back to us, hasn't he?'

'He certainly has,' said Mr Ellis.

By the time morning arrived, Mr Ellis had done some serious thinking. He had spent half the night discussing plans with his wife. They had a big new family staying at the hotel, and that meant a lot of extra work. This time they would really have to train Siggy to do some of it.

'After all,' said Mr Ellis, 'it wasn't his fault that he put the washing-up in the washing machine.'

'Maybe not,' his wife smiled.

'We'll train him to be a waiter. We always need extra hands when it comes to dishing up food. Tim and Zoe will be back at school, so they won't be able to help much longer.

The big plans were put into operation as soon as Sigurd appeared downstairs. Everybody was already at breakfast and Mr Ellis had warned them that Sigurd was going to help. 'Please be patient. He has a lot to learn.'

The smallest Johnson child poked his father's leg. 'This is going to be fun, Dad!'

Siggy appeared with two plates of scrambled egg and toast.

'That's for Mr and Mrs Johnson,' said Mr Ellis. 'Now, watch me, Siggy.' Mr Ellis carried a plate over to Mrs Tibblethwaite and put it in front of her. Sigurd grinned and took his plates across to the Johnsons. He tipped the contents on to the place mats. *Ssplopp!*

'Oh dear,' murmured Mrs Johnson.

'Siggy, you have to leave it on the plates,' explained Mr Ellis.

The Viking shook his big hairy head. 'No, make plaps dirty. No want dirty plaps.'

'It's okay, it doesn't matter if they get dirty. We always keep our food on the plates. Understand?'

'I understand,' said Siggy and he began to pick up the scrambled egg with his fingers and smear it back on the plates. The smallest Johnson tittered.

'He's funny,' he said.

'He's yukky,' the oldest one said, with some disgust.

'Sorry about this,' said Mr Ellis hastily. He pulled Sigurd into the corner of the room and started hissing instructions at him. Mrs Tibblethwaite tapped Mr Ellis on the shoulder.

'Let me do this. You get back to the kitchen. I'll soon have him under control.'

Mr Ellis retired gratefully to the kitchen, while Mrs Tibblethwaite slung a tea-towel over one arm and grabbed the Viking with the other. 'Now, watch me,' she ordered, and Sigurd followed her like a lamb.

Mr and Mrs Ellis and Tim and Zoe watched spellbound from the kitchen. 'You know, I do believe the old girl is quite enjoying herself,' said Mr Ellis. 'They make quite a pair, don't they, Penny?'

'She's a bit like a Viking warrior herself,'

his wife suggested. 'I'll be sad when she goes. She's been so helpful – more like one of the staff than a guest.

Mr Ellis smiled. 'Maybe everything is going to be all right after all. Perhaps Siggy will bring us good luck.'

'He's brought us a cow already,' Tim pointed out.

Zoe started to laugh.

7 Vanishing Act

Mrs Tibblethwaite was having remarkable success with Sigurd. She bossed him about like nobody's business, but the Viking smiled and laughed and nodded. He was soon well on his way to becoming a star waiter. Meanwhile Mrs Tibblethwaite was often to be seen wearing Sigurd's helmet. She looked quite the part.

The two weeks of Mrs Tibblethwaite's stay passed all too quickly. Mr and Mrs Ellis did not want the stout lady to go, as she had proved so helpful around the hotel. Tim and Zoe were both very fond of her because although she often had a strict and bossy manner, her heart was as soft as a king-size duvet.

And when Sigurd discovered that Mrs Tibblethwaite was leaving, he went to pieces completely. He tore at his hair, stamped up and down the stairs, frightened all the guests with his shouts and raging. Nobody understood a word he said: it was all in his own tongue. He would not lift a finger to help in the hotel. In short, the Viking had gone on strike.

Mrs Tibblethwaite was upset as well. She did not like to see Sigurd so unhappy, so she sat upstairs in her bedroom and tried to knit a jumper to take her mind off everything. The idea did not seem to work very well, as she ended up with the only jumper in the world that had three arms, no neck and a sock attached to one sleeve.

'Can't Mrs Tibblethwaite stay?' pleaded Zoe.

'It's really up to her,' explained Mrs Ellis.

'Can't she work here?' Zoe went on. Her mother stopped and looked at her in surprise.

'I don't know, Zoe. It never occurred to me. I don't suppose she would want to work here. She's got her own home, hasn't she?'

Even so, Mrs Ellis became very thoughtful after Zoe's suggestion, and decided she would talk to her husband about it as soon as possible. But there were other problems that needed seeing to first. All the chickens had disappeared from the kitchen table.

Mrs Ellis was certain she had taken three chickens from the fridge, ready to roast for lunch. When she couldn't see them, she decided her husband must already have put them in the oven to roast. When Mr Ellis couldn't find them in the fridge *he* had thought *she* must have put them in the oven.

It was now almost lunchtime, and they

both went to the oven to get the chickens. But the chickens weren't there. They had quite disappeared. Mr and Mrs Ellis looked at each other and said the same thing at the same time. 'Sigurd!'

They raced upstairs to his room, where they found the Viking moping on his bed. Mr Ellis hauled him to his feet. 'Chickens! What have you done with all the chickens?'

'Chickens,' repeated Sigurd. It was not a word he knew.

'Yes – chickens!' roared Mr Ellis frantically. He began to strut up and down the room with his fists tucked under his armpits and his elbows waggling. 'Parrk parrk paarkk!'

Sigurd's eyes grew wider and wider. He took off his helmet and scratched his head. Mrs Ellis hurriedly joined her husband. 'Parrkk puk-puk-pukpuk-puk parrkk!'

'Chickens!' cried Sigurd suddenly with a big smile, and he nodded feverishly.

'Thank goodness he understands,' panted Mr Ellis. But the Viking was now on his hands and knees, and had begun to crawl round the room.

'Woof wuff-wuff rrrrroooff!' Sigurd looked up at Mrs Ellis with his tongue hanging from his mouth. 'Rrrroooffff!'

'I don't believe it. He thinks this is a game,' moaned Mr Ellis. He grabbed Sigurd and pulled him on to his feet. 'Sigurd, chickens, where are they? We want to eat. Eat chickens. Lunchtime. Understand?'

'Ah, chickens. Yum-yums. I give to gods for offering. I give chickens to gods in Valhalla. I say, Oh Gods be good and Mrs Dufflecoat no go away.'

'WHERE ARE THE CHICKENS!' screamed Mr Ellis.

Sigurd paused and regarded Mr Ellis coolly. 'I show you,' he said calmly, and marched downstairs. He took them outside and pointed up to the porch roof. This had a triangular front, with a wooden spike at each corner. There was a farm-fresh oven-ready chicken stuck on each spike.

Mr Ellis was about to break into a war

dance when he saw the expression on
Sigurd's face. The Viking was gazing
upwards, his eyes half closed, his arms
raised to the heavens.

'Hear me, Odin!' the Viking cried.
'Hear me, Thor! Hear me all the gods in
Valhalla! Take my small offering and
speak to the heart of Mrs Dufflecoat so
she no go away. Speak to the hearts of Mr
Ellis and Mrs Ellis and Tim and Zoe,
who look after me, so they no send Mrs
Dufflecoat.' Sigurd slowly lowered his
arms.

Mrs Ellis gave a small nod and led
Sigurd back indoors. 'I'm sorry,' she
murmured. 'I didn't understand. Go back

upstairs, Sigurd, and we'll cook beefburgers instead.'

Mr Ellis was suddenly taken by an idea. He went straight to Mrs Tibblethwaite, explained the problem and asked her how she would solve it. Mrs Tibblethwaite looked him in the eye and said that the answer was perfectly obvious: 'You offer me a job and I say yes, then I stay here and everyone is happy.' And that was how Mrs Tibblethwaite came to work at The Viking Hotel.

As for the chickens, they stayed up on the porch roof for a very long time. Zoe explained that it was quite normal for Vikings to make offerings like that: 'Usually it was a pig or cow, I think. We learned about it at school.'

Whether it was the chickens on the porch roof, Sigurd or Mrs Tibblethwaite, nobody could be sure – but more and more people wanted to come and stay at The Viking Hotel. The hotel was soon doing great business, with all rooms full and booked for months to come.

The summer season ended with the great Flotby Viking Carnival. People all over the town had been preparing for weeks. It was a grand event, with parades along the streets, bands playing and a Viking Feast in the evening. There was dancing too.

Sigurd was like a small child. When he first saw the streets filled with Vikings, he thought Ulric Blacktooth had found him at last. He sat at the front window, watching with a pensive, faraway look in his eye. Zoe sat down beside him. She thought he would be excited and happy, today of all days. This was quite unexpected.

'You're thinking about home, aren't you, Siggy?'

'Hedeby,' grunted the Viking. Seeing all the people dressed like Vikings made his heart ache. Zoe left him to think alone.

Later in the evening they all went down to the harbour, where the grand feast and dance were to take place. Riding the waves in the harbour was a small boat, all done up like a Viking longship. It had shields along the sides and a striped sail. It even had a dragon's head prow (made from painted egg-boxes). Sigurd gazed at it with a curious smile and said, 'Baby boat,' which made everyone laugh. They went into the dance and left Siggy standing by the harbour, looking out to sea.

'He'll be all right,' said Tim.

'I'll go and have a word with him,' said Mrs Tibblethwaite. 'I'll see if I can get him to come and have a dance.' She set off along the harbour wall.

It was over an hour later that Mr Ellis suddenly realised he hadn't seen either Sigurd or Mrs Tibblethwaite come into the hall. Everyone had finished eating already, and there was no sign of them. His heart missed a beat as the truth came to him. 'Zoe, Tim, Penny! Quick, follow me!'

They pushed through the dancing crowds and out into the warm summer air. A brief glance at the harbour told them all they needed to know. The Viking longship had gone. They raced along the harbour wall and stared out across the dark sea.

'Nothing,' muttered Mr Ellis. 'I can't see a thing.'

'There! Over there, right on the horizon!' yelled Zoe. Far, far out to sea was a tiny sail. They watched it as long as possible, until it became a speck and then nothing.

The Ellises walked back to the hotel in a deep silence. On the porch steps they stopped and looked up at three very tatty old chickens.

'Give them a safe voyage, Odin,' said Mr Ellis quietly, and they went inside.

It was well past midnight when there was a loud knock on the front door. Mr Ellis went down in his dressing gown. Outside were two extremely wet figures. One was short and stout, the other was tall and hairy.

'We went round and round,' grinned Sigurd.

'He can't sail for toffee,' giggled Mrs

Tibblethwaite. 'He's totally hopeless. First of all . . .'

'He lost an oar,' butted in Mr Ellis. 'Don't tell me.'

'Big waves, very wet,' said Sigurd. 'Sail come down.'

'He was underneath, of course,' Mrs Tibblethwaite put in. 'Then he struggled to get out and he couldn't see what he was doing and kicked me overboard . . .'

'Gurgle-gurgle,' grinned Sigurd. 'Sail go dropsy-flopsy. Mrs Dufflecoat make big splash. She make very, very, *very* big splash.'

'Yes, well that's quite enough of that, Sigurd. You made a big splash, too.' Mrs Tibblethwaite turned back to Mr Ellis. 'He fell in as well, of course.'

'Gurgle-gurgle,' added Mr Ellis. 'Come on inside, the pair of you.' He began to switch on the hotel lights. 'Penny! Zoe! Tim! Come downstairs. We have some important guests who have just arrived.'

Sigurd stood in the hallway, with a large puddle of sea-water collecting round his feet. 'Tomorrow I make offering to thank gods in Valhalla for safe return,' he said.

'That will be fine, Sigurd,' said Mr Ellis. 'You can have a slice of bacon and no more. We haven't got any pigs, sheep or cows, so a slice of bacon will have to do.'

Sigurd stood and grinned at everyone like a huge, happy child. Suddenly he grabbed Mrs Tibblethwaite and gave her an enormous kiss. 'Sigurd like Mrs Dufflecoat. Like very much.'

'Oh – Siggy!' Mrs Tibblethwaite had turned bright red.

'Me love you!' declared Sigurd, with his idiotic smile. Then he grabbed her once more.

'All right, that's enough,' said Mr Ellis. 'Stop it at once. Time we ended all this.'

Choosing a brilliant book
can be a tricky business...
but not any more

www.puffin.co.uk

The best selection of books at your fingertips

So get clicking!

Searching the site is easy – you'll find
what you're looking for at the click of a mouse,
from great authors to brilliant books and more!

Read more in Puffin

For complete information about books available from Puffin – and Penguin – and how to order them, contact us at the appropriate address below. Please note that for copyright reasons the selection of books varies from country to country.

www.puffin.co.uk

In the United Kingdom: Please write to Dept EP, Penguin Books Ltd,
Bath Road, Harmondsworth, West Drayton, Middlesex UB7 0DA

In the United States: Please write to Penguin Putnam Inc., P.O. Box 12289,
Dept B, Newark, New Jersey 07101–5289 or call 1–800–788–6262

In Canada: Please write to Penguin Books Canada Ltd,
10 Alcorn Avenue, Suite 300, Toronto, Ontario M4V 3B2

In Australia: Please write to Penguin Books Australia Ltd,
P.O. Box 257, Ringwood, Victoria 3134

In New Zealand: Please write to Penguin Books (NZ) Ltd,
Private Bag 102902, North Shore Mail Centre, Auckland 10

In India: Please write to Penguin Books India Pvt Ltd,
11 Panscheel Shopping Centre, Panscheel Park, New Delhi 110 017

In the Netherlands: Please write to Penguin Books Netherlands bv,
Postbus 3507, NL–1001 AH Amsterdam

In Germany: Please write to Penguin Books Deutschland GmbH,
Metzlerstrasse 26, 60594 Frankfurt am Main

In Spain: Please write to Penguin Books S. A., Bravo Murillo 19,
1° B, 28015 Madrid

In Italy: Please write to Penguin Italia s.r.l.,
Via Felice Casati 20, I–20124 Milano

In France: Please write to Penguin France S. A.,
17 rue Lejeune, F–31000 Toulouse

In Japan: Please write to Penguin Books Japan, Ishikiribashi Building,
2–5–4, Suido, Bunkyo-ku, Tokyo 112

In South Africa: Please write to Longman Penguin Southern Africa (Pty) Ltd,
Private Bag X08, Bertsham 2013